KIDS CAN COPE

Say Hi
When You're Shy

by Gill Hasson

illustrated by Sarah Jennings

Franklin Watts
First published in Great Britain in 2020
by The Watts Publishing Group

All rights reserved.

Copyright in the text Gill Hasson 2020
Copyright in the illustrations Franklin Watts 2020

Series Editor: Jackie Hamley
Series Designer: Cathryn Gilbert

A CIP catalogue record for this book is
available from the British Library.

ISBN 978 1 4451 6613 1 (hbk)
ISBN 978 1 4451 6614 8 (pbk)

Printed in China

Franklin Watts
An imprint of
Hachette Children's Group
Part of The Watts Publishing Group
Carmelite House
50 Victoria Embankment
London EC4Y 0DZ

An Hachette UK Company
www.hachette.co.uk

www.franklinwatts.co.uk

FSC
www.fsc.org
MIX
Paper from
responsible sources
FSC® C104740

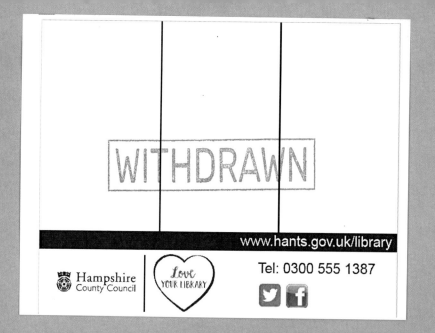

Say Hi When You're Shy

by Gill Hasson

illustrated by Sarah Jennings

Turn the page to read about ways to feel more confident with other people.

Feeling shy?

What does it mean to be shy?

Do you get shy? It's not just you!
Everyone feels shy sometimes – even grown-ups!
We feel shy when we're not sure what to say or do around other people. We can feel nervous when we try something new, or until we get used to doing something.

What if I do it wrong and they all laugh at me?

Sometimes, being shy can mean we are good at watching others and thinking things through.

5

How do you feel when you're shy?

When you're feeling shy, you might get worried or even scared. You might get embarrassed and feel uncomfortable. You might worry about looking silly to other people.

Perhaps your face gets hot and your heart starts thumping. Your legs go all shaky and your stomach feels all fluttery.

Sometimes, you might feel sad or lonely because you want to join in with other children but your shyness holds you back.

Other times, you might just want to be on your own but you're worried that this will upset other people, or that they won't invite you to join in next time.

What happens when you feel shy?

When you're with other children, you might be quiet and not say much to them. Perhaps you watch others play, but you don't join in.

You might feel shy around grown-ups, too.
Maybe you find it difficult to speak up,
so you mumble, whisper, or say nothing at all.

It can feel like your tongue is tied. You might look at the ground and think that you just want to shrink or be left alone.

Hello, Leo.
How is your new school?

Erm...

9

It's okay to feel shy!

If you often feel shy, it might take time for you to feel comfortable in new situations and with new people.

Maybe you like to watch for a while before you feel ready to join in.

And sometimes you just might like being on your own and playing alone.

That's okay!

There could, though, be times when you do want to join in,
but you don't know how to get past your shyness.
You're not sure what to say or do.
And this might mean you feel left out.

Come and sit with us!

Don't hide because you're shy! There are things
you can do. You can learn to be more confident
and comfortable around other people.

Knowing what to say

Think about how you feel around people who you're not shy with; people you know well like your mum or dad, a brother or sister, or a good friend.

When you're around friends and family you do feel comfortable with, you talk clearly in a voice they can hear.

Pass the ketchup, please!

You feel relaxed and safe telling them what you do and don't want. You ask them things and you answer their questions. You're friendly and you don't have to think about how to talk to them or what to say.

You can learn to do this more easily with other people, too.

Taking steps to feel less shy

To start with, think of some things you feel too shy to do or say and write them down. Choose one thing that you're just a bit uncomfortable about doing.

Try to come up with ideas for how to do this without feeling so shy. There are ideas in this book to help you. Practise doing that one thing until you feel better about it. Then move on to the next thing on your list.

Jenna wrote down things that she was shy about doing. There were some things she felt a bit shy about, and other things she felt really shy about.
Then Jenna started on the first thing she felt a bit worried about and came up with some ideas to help her feel happier about it.

- Asking to join in with a game
- Going to a party
- Standing up in class
- Telling someone I don't want to do something
- Paying for something in a shop.
- Talking to my friends' parents
- Asking my teacher a question.

Invite a friend to your home

If you feel awkward around other children, you might find it easier to be with just one person rather than lots at the same time. So you could try starting with one friend.

Sometimes, it can be easier to be with a new friend in your own home where you feel most comfortable and relaxed. Perhaps you could invite another child to your home to play for a couple of hours. Before your friend arrives, think about some things you could do together that you might both enjoy.

Once your friend is there, try to make him or her feel welcome.

Ask what your friend would like to play. You could suggest some of the things to do together that you thought of earlier.

Plan ahead for parties

Sometimes, you'll want to go to places where there will be lots of people. This can be fun — but it can be scary, too.

Alfie was worried about feeling shy at his friend Holly's party. There would be other children there that he didn't know.

Alfie and his mum decided to practise what he could do. They set up an imaginary party with Alfie's toys and pretended that one of the toys was shy. Alfie showed the toy what to do and say.

If you are worried about being shy at a party or another event, ask a grown-up or a friend to help you plan a few simple things you could say. This can help you feel more prepared and happier about going. Other people might also be feeling shy there, just like you. Maybe you'll even help someone else feel less shy!

Join something you like doing

Sometimes, you might find it easier not to feel shy if you can join in with something you really like doing. You don't have to do something on your own.

You might feel better about joining a club or going to a new activity if you went with someone you know. Ask a friend if they'd like to go with you.

Perhaps you like doing gymnastics, football, basketball or cricket.
Or dancing and singing.
Does your school have some after school clubs?
Maybe there's an art or games club you could go along to.

When you join in with activities like these, you already have something to do and talk about with other children.

You might need to go a few times before you feel less shy.
That's fine.

When you feel shy around adults

Talking to grown-ups isn't always easy.
A good idea is to ask someone else to help you
think of some simple things you could say in
different situations.

Lizzie and her grandma practised ways Lizzie
could talk to adults. Each time, she remembered
to look at the other person and talk clearly
in a voice the other person could hear.

Excuse me, can I stroke your dog?

23

Saying what you do and don't want

There are some situations where it can be really difficult to say what you do or don't want.

But that's my ball!

You might find it hard to say that you don't like something or you don't want to do something.

Or that you don't understand something and need some help.

You might worry that others won't listen to you or might make fun of what you say.

Practise speaking up

Even when it's hard, sometimes you need to speak up!

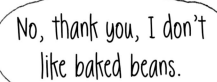 No, thank you, I don't like baked beans.

Speaking up means saying what you do or don't want in a polite but firm way.

I'm not sure how to do the homework. Please can you tell me what I need to do?

If there's something that is important to you but that you find difficult to speak up about, you could ask a grown-up or a friend to help you practise saying it. It can help to practise in the mirror on your own, too.

Build up your courage

What you need and what you do or don't want matters.
If you don't want to do something or you need help,
you can say something!

You will need a bit of courage. This means doing something
even though you feel a little bit scared.

You can tell yourself, "I can do this" and "It will be okay".
Take a big breath and then as soon as you breathe out,
look at the other person. In a voice the other person can hear,
say what you do or don't want, or what you need.

I can do this!
It will be okay!

You might be surprised at how good it feels to speak up.
And each time you speak out, you might feel
more and more confident.

Say Hi When You're Shy

We feel shy when we're not sure what to say or do around other children and grown-ups. It might take a little while for you to warm up and feel comfortable in new situations and with new people. And sometimes you might just prefer to be on your own. That's fine! But when you do want to join in and talk to other people, you can learn to be more confident and comfortable. Here's a reminder:

- Ask a grown-up or a friend to help you plan a few simple things you could say in situations where you feel shy. Practise together until it feels easier for you.

- Invite a new friend to your home, make him or her feel welcome and do some things together that you'll both enjoy.

- Think of an activity you really like doing that you could join in with other children. Ask another friend if they'd like to go to it with you.

- When you need to speak up, tell yourself, "I can do this". Take a big breath, look at the other person and, in a voice the other person can hear, say what you do or don't want.

And remember, you can always start by saying "hi!"

Now you know it's okay to feel shy.

And you know how to help yourself feel more comfortable around others.

Activities

These drawing and writing activities can help you to think more about how to feel less shy around other people.

- Draw your shy face. Then draw your friendly face.

- Kira is worried about feeling shy when she goes to her friend's picnic. What do you think Kira could do to help her feel less worried about it? Write Kira a letter with some ideas about what she can do or say at the picnic.

- Anton is worried about standing up in class next week when it's his turn to do show-and-tell. Write him a letter with an idea for what he could do that can help him feel more prepared and less shy.

- Think of a situation where you often feel shy. Draw a picture of yourself in that situation, looking confident and happy.

- Ask a grown-up what they were shy about when they were a child. Ask them what happened that helped them feel less shy. Draw a picture or write a story about it.

- Write down some things you can say to yourself to help you have courage when you need to speak up about what you do or don't want.

Notes for teachers, parents and carers

As a parent, you'll want your child to feel at ease with others and to have confidence in social situations, so you may feel frustrated if your child is slower to warm up, shy, and gets worried about joining in with other children or talking to adults. If you are concerned that your child is too shy, it's important that you avoid labelling your child as shy or nervous, either directly to them or when talking about them to others. Labels stick and lead to a self-fulfilling prophecy. If you label your child as shy, you give them permission to stay in their shell.

Instead, give them other ways in which to think about themselves. You could say, for example,

"It's fine if it takes a little while for you to feel comfortable with new people."

"You like to listen to others and watch what's happening first before you join in."

"It's good that you talk easily with people you know well. People like our neighbour and..."

Try not to step in too much. Resist, for example, the urge to respond to a question an adult asks your child; instead, encourage your child to look at the adult and answer the question themselves.

Children need effective techniques and strategies to help them take control and feel in control. *Say Hi When You're Shy* explains ways in which your child can manage feeling shy. There's a range of strategies which you can help them with, for example helping your child rehearse ahead of time for a situation that makes them nervous, like going to a birthday party or meeting new people. You can also help them come up with ideas for activities they'd feel at ease with doing, with other children.

Although your child can read this book by themselves, it will be more helpful for both of you if you could read it together. You could talk about situations that you find daunting and how you manage them: For example, "Sometimes I feel worried about speaking up at work, but I take a deep breath and say something and it's always okay."

There are lots of talking points. Ask your child questions such as: Have you felt like that? What do you think of that idea? How could that work for you? Talk about the characters in the illustrations, too.

Having read the book and helped your child identify some strategies that could work for them, give them the opportunity to manage the situations at their own pace and with your support. With time, patience, support and encouragement from you, your child can learn to cope with and be more confident with others. If though, their shyness, worries and fears are frequently causing them distress and leading them to avoid everyday situations and miss out, then it's worth seeking more advice, so do approach your doctor and ask for help. You can also get advice from youngminds.org.uk or call their Parents Helpline on 0808 802 5544.